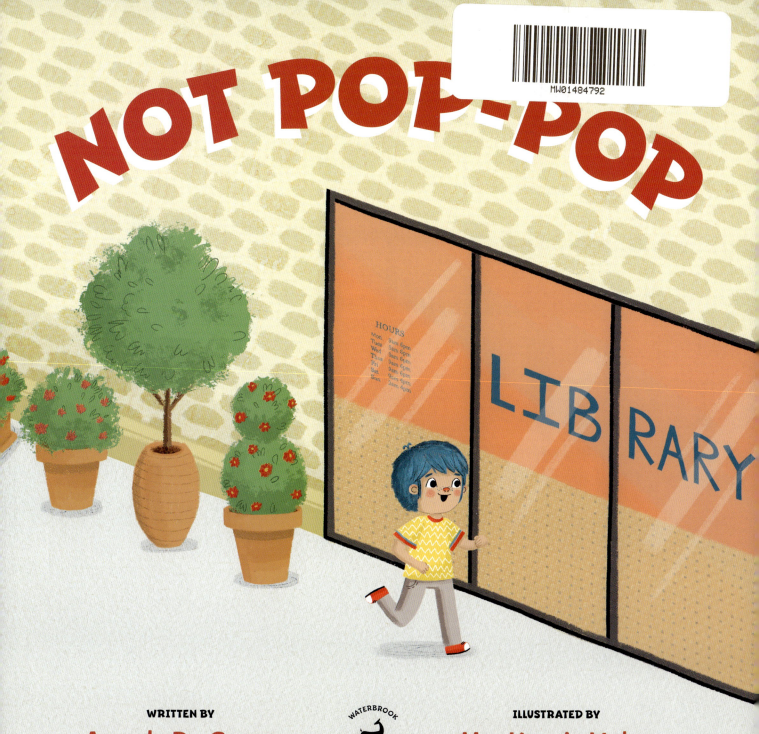

NOT POP-POP

WRITTEN BY

Angela De Groot

WATERBROOK

ILLUSTRATED BY

MacKenzie Haley

Return Books Here ↑

I ♥ Books

Yay! It's library day.
The doors *SWISH* open.
I slide my old books down the chute.

THONK!

I *ZOOM* to find new ones.

I *ZIG* by crawling babies

and *ZAG* past knitting nanas until . . .

PLOP!

I land in my favorite spot.

I *FLIP* the pages,
  then look up and see . . .

Same eyes.
Same beard.
Same bushy brows.

"Pop-Pop?!"

I jump up.

I run.

That's *not* my pop-pop!

Yay! It's sing-along time.
Guitar Lady strums and sings.
We stomp. We shout.
We shake it all about.

When our song ends, we hear . . .

SNORE!

Not Pop-Pop is napping, feet up like my pop-pop.
My pop-pop's socks are always snow-bright white.

While Mom checks out our books, I look at the special bookshelf.
"Northern lights are spectacular!" Not Pop-Pop says.
I like his rumbly voice. It's just like my pop-pop's.

"Mom, what does *spectacular* mean?"

"'Eye-catching.' Like a rainbow."

There are no books in Mom's bag today.
It's full of cans! *Tuna? Tomatoes?*

"Who are they for?" I ask.

"For people who don't have enough to eat."

The library is quiet.
Except for that rumbly voice.

Not Pop-Pop is talking to himself.
Like my pop-pop does . . . but louder.
Everyone looks, then looks away.

"Vagrant," Frowny-Face Lady says.

"Mom, what's a vagrant?"

"It's what *some* people call someone without a home."

Restrooms

Checkout

I do puzzles.

I play with trains. *TOOT TOOT!*

Until . . . uh-oh!

I *CHOO-CHOO* to the restroom.

"I can go in by myself," I tell Mom.

But when I get to the sink, Not Pop-Pop is brushing his teeth.

I'll wash my hands later.

While Mom picks a movie, I play on the computer.
Not Pop-Pop is playing too.

CLICK CLICK goes Not Pop-Pop's mouse.
CLICK CLICK goes his tongue.

My pop-pop does that too sometimes.

It's time to go.

"Look!" I whisper to Mom.

"That's what they're for," Mom says.

"Oh."

I hope Not Pop-Pop likes yucky beans.

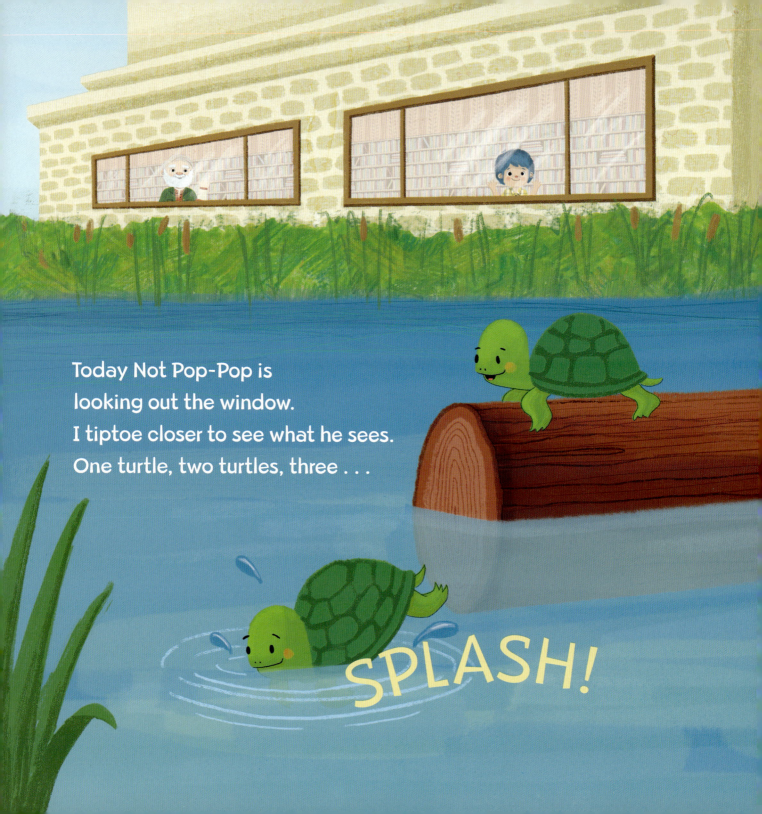

Today Not Pop-Pop is
looking out the window.
I tiptoe closer to see what he sees.
One turtle, two turtles, three . . .

SPLASH!

Now it's number four's turn in the sun.

Out in the parking lot, Not Pop-Pop opens his car door.

"I'll move it," he tells Security Man.

"Bum," Security Man mutters as he walks away.

"Mom, what's a bum?"

"*Not* a nice word."

Rain *PLINK-PLONKS*
against the windows,
SPLITTER-SPLATS into the pond.
There are no turtles today
and that makes me sad.

Not Pop-Pop too, I think.
My eyes find his.
I finger wave.
He nods.

"I need a volcano book," I tell Mom.
We walk past a poster. Those sneakers
look like Not Pop-Pop's.

"Mom, what's it say?"

"'Compassion.' It means 'be kind, and help make the world a better place.'"

Checkout

Volcanoes

After Mom tucks me in, I try to sleep,
but words bounce in my head.

Spectacular.

Compassion.

Vagrant?

Bum?

He's not *my* pop-pop, but . . .
he's *someone's* pop-pop.

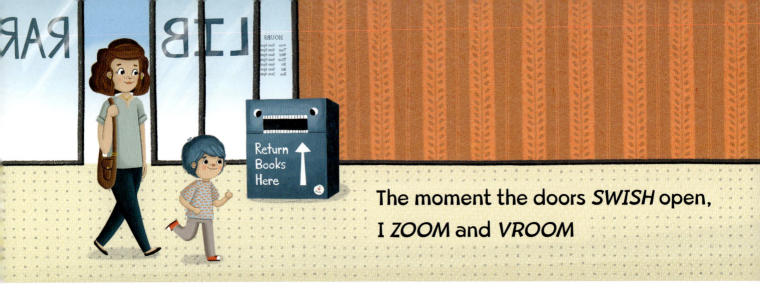

The moment the doors *SWISH* open,
I *ZOOM* and *VROOM*

until . . . I find a just-right one.

Then I *RACE* through the library to find him.

"It's spectacular,"
I tell Not Pop-Pop.

He smiles.

"I'm Brian," I say.

"I'm George," he says.

George loves books.

Like my pop-pop.
Like me.

Understanding Homelessness

What is homelessness?

Some people live in houses. Some people live in apartments. But some people don't have a place they can call home. They live outside or in their car or in a shelter with other people. A person who doesn't have a home is experiencing homelessness.

Why does homelessness happen?

There are a lot of reasons a person could be experiencing homelessness. Sometimes bad storms, fires, or wars destroy people's homes. Sometimes housing is too expensive. When a person doesn't make enough money, loses their job, has a disability, or is too sick to work, they can't pay for a home. Some people can stay with friends or family, but not everyone has a community to help them, which is why there are shelters or camps they can stay in until they find a new home.

How Can We Help?

Some people experiencing homelessness are adults. Some are kids. Some are moms, dads, or pop-pops. The most important way to help people experiencing homelessness is to treat them the way you like to be treated: with kindness and respect. Many cities are trying to end homelessness by building more homes that cost less money and by paying people enough money to afford a home of their own. And there are ways that you can help too!

- Donate toys, hats, gloves, games, art supplies, and other new or gently used items to a shelter.

- Make a poster to hang at your school or library.

- Write a kindness card to put in donation packages and goody bags.

- Pack goody bags with socks, protein bars, bottled water, and a travel-size toothbrush and toothpaste to hand out to people in need.

- Volunteer with a caregiver at a food bank or soup kitchen.

- Remember, words have power. Choose them carefully. Are they kind and respectful?

You may be one person. You may be young, but just like in the story, you can make a big difference in the life of a person in need. You can be a positive part of their day.

For Parents, Caregivers, and Teachers

Children are observant and curious. They ask questions that don't have easy answers. Although topics like homelessness have nuances that are hard for young children to understand, it's never too early to help them develop into global citizens. Here are some ways you can support children's learning:

- Model empathy. Express how you feel about other people's struggles. Children will follow your example and learn to treat people experiencing homelessness with understanding and respect.

- Use kid-friendly words and keep explanations simple. Ask questions to gauge what they already know about the topic; then supplement their understanding with additional information. For example, "Why do you think that person sleeps in a box? Yes, it's sad that houses are too expensive for some people."

- Address concerns and provide reassurance. Learning that some people don't have a place to stay is upsetting, and children may worry about this happening to their own family. Assure them that there are organizations that help house and feed families struggling with homelessness. If you are a parent or guardian, help your children feel safe by explaining what your plan of action would be if your family were at risk.

- Encourage action. Help children find ways to be part of the solution. For ideas on how your family, school, or community can support people experiencing homelessness, check out the "How Can We Help?" section.

Let's show children how compassion can build a better world.

Published in the United States by WaterBrook, an imprint of
Random House, a division of Penguin Random House LLC.

WaterBrook and colophon are registered trademarks of
Penguin Random House LLC.

ISBN 978-0-593-57892-6
Ebook ISBN 978-0-593-57893-3

The Library of Congress catalog record is available
at https://lccn.loc.gov/2022013221.

Printed in China

waterbrookmultnomah.com

9 8 7 6 5 4 3 2 1

First Edition

Book and cover design by Ashley Tucker

Most WaterBrook books are available at special quantity
discounts for bulk purchase for premiums, fundraising, and corporate
and educational needs by organizations, churches, and businesses.
Special books or book excerpts also can be created to fit specific needs.
For details, contact specialmarketscms@penguinrandomhouse.com.